OH PAUL!

Mary Rayner

Illustrated by
THE AUTHOR

HEINEMANN   LONDON

William Heinemann Ltd
Michelin House
81 Fulham Road, London SW3 6RB

LONDON MELBOURNE
JOHANNESBURG AUCKLAND

First published 1988
© Mary Rayner 1988

ISBN 0 434 93052 0
Printed in Hong Kong
by Mandarin Offset

A school pack of BANANAS 25-30
is available from
Heinemann Educational Books
ISBN 0 435 00104 3

1

AND MAY I remind you, children,' said the Headmaster, 'that it's just two weeks till Fletchley's May Fair. That's on the Saturday, but the Friday before will be a dressing-up day for all of you. I want you each to come to school as your favourite character out of a book. Then we've arranged for you to be at the Fair in your costumes to join in the procession with all the floats. There'll be prizes for the best costumes at the end of the afternoon.'

Paul was not listening. He was sitting

with everyone else on the wooden floor of the hall, seeing if he could curl his tongue right over so that it was upside-down. He had already discovered that he could make it touch the tip of his nose, which was more than anyone else in the playground had been able to do. Now he found that he could roll it up like a brandy snap inside his mouth, but it wouldn't turn over. It was an interesting problem, and he had almost done it when he found everyone round him standing up to leave the hall.

He scrambled to his feet and followed the line out through the door, along the passage, past the cloakroom and across the playground to Class 3H.

When everyone was there Miss Hornbeam said, 'Well, I hope we're all going to make a really good effort with the writing display.'

What writing display? Paul couldn't
remember anything about one. He
asked Jackie, who sat next to him.

'But Mr Wilson just told us, stupid,'
said Jackie. Paul looked blank. 'Oh
Paul! Just now, in Assembly.'

'Oh,' said Paul. He was not all that
good at writing. His was large and
untidy. There would be things written
down the side of his exercise book like
*Try and get more than three words per
line, Paul*, and, in red ink, *Spelling,
Paul*! when he'd written *aslo*. An easy
thing to do, thought Paul, anybody

could see that it was meant to be *also*, and as long as people could understand what you meant, that seemed okay to him. That was what writing was *for*.

Miss Hornbeam was Brown Owl for the local Brownie pack. More like a barn owl, thought Paul. She had whitish hair and starey eyes and big hands which she clapped when 3H was getting too noisy. And sometimes she'd swoop down on you even when you were doing something quite mouselike and quiet, such as making a teepee out of your coloured pencils with a rubber band, and haul you out in front of the class.

Paul was interested in animals and wild life. It was all still new to him. His Mum and Dad had moved to Fletchley from London, and he had come to Fletchley Primary when he was nearly seven, the summer before.

One of the first things that had happened to Paul had been the matter of the tadpoles. Paul had been told to look after them, help change their water every so often, see that they had enough weed to eat. Then he was to make sure there was a stone for them to climb out onto when they began to grow legs and breathe. Paul longed for them to turn into frogs. There hadn't been any frogs in London. He had wanted to find out when they could breathe air. They were taking an awful long time to grow legs. He had taken them out of the tank and put them in a double row on blotting paper next to it, and then unluckily the bell had gone for the end of the afternoon and Paul had rushed out to play football with the others.

Next morning when he came into school there were all the tadpoles, lying very still and quiet on the blotting paper, and there hadn't been time to slip them back into the tank before Miss Hornbeam had noticed them.

He had been made to go up onto the platform in front of the whole school, and Mr Wilson had made a long and terrible speech about cruelty to helpless creatures. Paul had not had a chance to tell anyone that he'd only been trying to *help* them. Since then he wasn't even allowed to feed the gerbils. It was awful. They'd even telephoned his Mum.

Now Jackie was saying 'All our writing will be put out so that everyone in Fletchley can see it at the May Fair. Not just our Mums and Dads. To show everybody what a good school this is, so they won't all go and send their children to other schools.'

'Is that what they do?' asked Paul, surprised.

'Everybody comes to Fletchley Primary to begin with, and then lots get taken away and driven to other schools miles away.'

'Why?' asked Paul. 'This school's all right.'

'*I* know,' said Jackie, 'but *they* don't.'

'It's a pity it's writing,' said Paul

gloomily. 'If it was football I could show them.'

Amanda leaned across the table. 'I'm going to another school when I'm bigger,' she said. 'A boarding school. My Mummy says so. And I'm going to win the fancy dress competition.'

'How d'you know?' asked Edward, twisting round from the next table.

'Because. Because I just know,' said Amanda, sounding very pleased with herself.

Paul saw Miss Hornbeam coming nearer, nudged Jackie, and bent over his book, looking at the pages hard. Nobody said anything for a while.

2

IT WAS THURSDAY, nearly two weeks later. Paul still had not managed a piece of writing that Miss Hornbeam thought good enough for the display. She had told him to get one done that evening without fail. Paul lay on his bed and sucked his pencil. In front of him was a blank sheet of paper on top of a book. Paul wrote *Why I wood lik a rabit by Paul Stephens.*

He thought about the next-door rabbits. How their noses moved up and down, and the way they huddled together with their heads tucked back into their shoulders when it was windy or cold. The babies were best, with their little ears. There was a new lot, born last week. Old Tom Drew had said he could have one, but his mother had said no,

he was too young to look after a pet.
She didn't say so, but he just knew she
was thinking about the tadpoles.

Paul kicked his feet angrily against
the bedding. He crossed out what he had
just written, and put *How to loke after
pets*. Underneath he wrote *You got to
no what they nead. Rabits nead gras or
cabaj, cats nead milk or fish. Gotes* – he

paused, chewing his pencil. Then he
wrote *eat any thing*. That's what Tom
Drew had told him.

He slipped off his bed and went to the
window. He could hear a cuckoo calling
from the blue haze of woodland beyond
the village. And he could see, in the
rough patch behind all their gardens
where Tom Drew kept his goats, the

white one, tied up on a long rope. In Tom Drew's garden next door Hans, the Dutch rabbit, was sitting up on his haunches with his ears up in startled V. Paul ran down the stairs, writing paper still clutched in one hand, and out through the back door. He climbed onto the top of a dustbin to watch Hans over the fence. For a long time he watched the rabbits nibbling the grass and moving about lazily in their run, until he heard his mother calling him in for bed.

Scrambling down, he let go of the piece of paper, and it skittered across the garden, coming to rest among some brambles against the far fence. Paul ran after it, and was just in time to grab hold of it before the wind took it again. It tore across the bottom corner. Paul looked at it. You could still read it, although it did look a bit dirty. Maybe he could get the dirt off with a rubber? He ran indoors.

3

PAUL WAS WOKEN early by the cuckoo calling again, nearer and louder; through his window the sun was bright, and he had never heard so many birds singing. Friday today, and the May Fair tomorrow. Then with a lurch he remembered: goodness, this was the day they had to go to school in fancy dress. Help! Paul jumped out of bed and hurried onto the landing.

He could hear his father splashing in the bathroom. In the bedroom Paul was surprised to see his mother already dressed; she was standing by the mirror doing her hair.

'Mum, I've got to have fancy dress. Now. Somebody out of a book.'

'Oh *Paul*! Why are you only telling me today?'

''Cos I only just remembered.'

She was cross. 'How can I possibly get you dressed up now? I've got to be at the Cross Keys early to make it extra clean and tidy for the May Fair.'

'I've got to have something,' said Paul. 'Miss Hornbeam said. Amanda's going to be Heidi, and Tom Drew's letting her borrow his goats, and

Marigold Melrose is coming to judge it
and open the Fair.'

'Not *the* Marigold Melrose?' said
Paul's father in surprise, coming in with
a towel round his shoulders. 'Off the
telly?'

'Yes,' said Paul. 'She's Amanda's
aunt.'

His mother dropped her hairbrush.
'What, Marigold Melrose out of
Legacy? Coming to Fletchley?'

'Yes,' said Paul, impatient. *Legacy*
was on twice a week, with repeats on
Sundays. Paul didn't watch it much, but

his Mum never missed it unless she had to be at the Cross Keys, and then she made sure to catch the repeat.

'Goodness,' she said. 'In that case I'd better be off sharpish. She might come into the Cross Keys; I'll have to make it all really sparkle. Ooh, Marigold Melrose! Fancy, I might speak to her!' She brushed her hair harder. 'Why didn't you say before? Why didn't I know? Everyone in the village must've known.'

'She's only just said she can come,' said Paul. 'Nobody knew. Amanda's Dad wrote to ask her but she was in America. She only just got back.'

'Just wait till I tell them,' said his Mum, snatching up her handbag and hurrying downstairs.

'What about my dressing-up?' Paul called after her.

'Oh *Paul*,' said his father, shaking his head, but he was half smiling. 'Here, take my old football scarf and socks. You can be a football supporter,' and he threw Paul the clothes.

Back in his room Paul put on a tee shirt and wound the green and yellow scarf round his neck. It looked terrific. He pulled on a pair of jeans and tried on the socks. They were much too big, and he couldn't get his trainers on over them. He stuffed them in his pocket, grabbed the page of writing and ran downstairs for a quick bowl of cereal before school.

4

THE PLAYGROUND WAS crowded with witches and spacemen and every kind of character. Paul saw Jackie in a black leotard, black tights and gum boots. She had a black paper tail, slanty eyes and black whiskers felt-tipped across her face.

'Hey,' said Paul, 'that's good. Puss in Boots!'

In the classroom Miss Hornbeam was kneeling on the floor in front of a cardboard box Dalek. The Dalek was shouting that it was too hot. 'We'll take it off just for now,' soothed Miss Hornbeam, 'don't worry.'

Paul said, 'Please, here's my writing.'

Miss Hornbeam was easing the box
upwards. 'Good, put it on the pile on
my desk, there's a good boy,' she said,
uncovering a red-faced Edward.

Amanda was sitting on her chair. She
was wearing a flower-embroidered
Swiss skirt and blouse, her hair in two
plaits instead of her usual bunches. She
looked very pretty and knew it.

'Where are the goats?' asked Jackie.

'Silly, I couldn't bring them into school,' said Amanda.

'I don't believe you've got any goats,' said Jackie.

'I have,' said Amanda.

'You haven't.'

'I bet you anything I'll win and you won't with your silly old welly boots. Marigold Melrose is my Aunty and she'll make sure I get the prize.'

Jackie glanced down at her boots and muttered, 'Don't suppose she even *is* your aunt.'

'She is.'

'Liar, liar,' chanted Jackie, and the others took it up. Miss Hornbeam clapped her hands for quiet.

'You'll see tomorrow,' hissed Amanda as they lined up to go into Assembly.

Miss Hornbeam's eyes swept along the line and halted at Paul. 'Who are you meant to be?'

'Er . . . my Dad said to be a football supporter.' Paul held out the socks. 'But –'

Miss Hornbeam cut him short. 'That's not out of a book. Oh *Paul*! When will you learn?' She looked at the socks, then took one, stretched the ribbed top wide and pulled it down on Paul's head as a cap. 'There, you can be an elf, from *The Elves and the Shoemaker*.' And she unwound the scarf and put it on her desk.

Paul felt his face burning. Amanda stifled a titter. Miss Hornbeam swept on down the line. 'There's no judging today anyway, this is just a sort of rehearsal for tomorrow when you'll all join in the procession with the lorries and floats. It's going to be a very important day for the school; you're all to be on your very best behaviour, and that goes for you too, Paul.'

5

LATE ON SATURDAY morning Paul put on the green tee shirt and a pair of old school trousers that were too short for him. If he'd got to be an elf he'd be a really *good* elf. His father had said he could cut pointy edges round the bottoms with scissors. They looked all right, Paul thought, pleased, as he posed

in front of the landing mirror. Miss
Hornbeam had suggested he take off his
shoes and socks for the final parade by
the Girl Guides' Tent, it would be grass
and he wouldn't hurt his feet. He pulled
on the green striped sock cap. His face,
round and pink and all too mortal-

looking, stared back at him from the mirror. Something more was needed, but what?

He couldn't ask his mother, she had gone along to the Cross Keys, and his father was mowing the front grass. Paul had an idea.

He went to the cupboard under the stairs and took out a tin of green shoe polish. He spread the polish over his face. It slid on easily. This was fun. Paul

rubbed it in all over, and down his neck and over his hands. And more on his feet.

Paul's father came back into the house. 'Phew,' he said, 'it's hot. That lawn should do, even for your Mum!' He grinned, and then caught sight of Paul. 'Oh Paul – ' he began and then checked himself. 'You look terrific.'

They had a quick bite to eat and then set off. Marigold Melrose was to open the Fair at two o'clock.

Fletchley had a long straight main street with a wide strip of green at either side. Usually the green was used for cricket or football, but today it looked quite different.

Slung across the main street was a banner, saying *May Fair*, and there were stalls with cakes and jams, stalls with vegetables, stalls with flowers, a

tent with Oxfam things, a tent with toys and games, and many more. There were coconut shies and tombolas and a trampoline, and at the far end of the green, lined up along the main street, Paul could see the lorries and floats waiting to start the procession.

Paul's father gave him some money. 'Here son, that's the Guide Tent, over there. Off you go and find your friends, I'm going along to the Cross Keys.'

Paul ran barefoot across the grass to the crowd of children by the Guide

Tent. There was a low platform in front
of the tent, and a big television van
parked behind it. The first person he
saw was Amanda, holding onto Tom
Drew's white goat. She was wearing her
Heidi clothes but she was nowhere near
as neat as the day before. The goat was
pulling and tugging, eager to look at
everything that was going on, and
Amanda's blouse was out of her skirt
and one plait was already undone.

Paul went up and patted the goat, and
it leaned towards him, sniffing at his

pockets. Paul went into the Guide Tent, where they were going to serve teas, to find a lump of sugar. All the writing from Fletchley Primary was pinned up on screens inside. Paul saw his page. It looked much dirtier and more torn now that it was beside all the others, and there seemed even less writing.

Paul took the sugar and dodged back out again as fast as he could. He put an arm round the goat's neck, holding the sugar under its nose. The goat took it, chomping it up with a sideways crunch and eyeing him for more.

'Now look what you've done,' said Amanda. There were green shoe-polishy smears on the goat's white neck.

'Sorry,' said Paul, but the goat didn't mind. It was shoving a friendly head against Paul's chest.

Miss Hornbeam swooped out of the

tent in her Brown Owl's uniform, clapped her hands and hooted, 'Time for the procession to start, over you go, children, to the floats.'

The goat was startled. It leapt sideways, jerking the rope out of Amanda's hand, and took off across the green.

'Quick,' shouted Paul, and ran after it. Amanda followed. The goat slowed up near a stall, stopped and put its head down to crop the grass. Paul grabbed

Amanda. 'Stay there, I'll try and sneak up on it.'

Amanda looked over her shoulder. Everyone from the school was walking towards the floats, and behind them strode Miss Hornbeam. 'I'm going to miss the procession,' Amanda wailed.

'Leave it to me,' said Paul. He heard Amanda shout 'Thanks,' as she ran after the others, but his eyes were on the goat.

6

PAUL CREPT FORWARDS. He was within a few feet of the rope which trailed behind the goat when it lifted its head and walked on. Paul watched paralysed as it went up to the cake stall, wrapped a long tongue round a fairy cake and ate it, paper and all. The

grey-haired lady behind the stall waved
her arms and shouted, and it jumped
backwards and cantered off again across
the green.

Paul panted after it. It was going
towards the line of the floats. Paul put
on a spurt and headed it off from the
road. It slowed down again a little way
off. Paul paused to regain his breath. He
heard Mr Wilson shout up to the
leading lorry driver 'Can't you hang on
a bit? Marigold Melrose should be here
any minute to open the Fair.'

'Sorry mate,' said the driver. 'Got to have this lorry back at the depot by six. Can't wait any longer. We'll go round the village and come back in a circle. Maybe she'll be here by then.'

Paul crept towards the goat, wriggling along on his stomach. Nearly. Ah! He made a dive forwards and grabbed the rope.

The goat plunged sideways again and the rope was twitched out of Paul's hand. He jumped to his feet and set off in pursuit. The goat went faster. It careered back the way it had come, and into one of the guy ropes of the Oxfam tent, bringing down one end in a billowing heap. Paul could hear muffled cries and see wild movements under the canvas. The goat ran on. So did Paul.

It slowed again by the vegetable stall and snuffed at the table of produce. Paul

tiptoed up and took the rope firmly in
one hand. Quickly he held out a
tenpenny piece. 'I'll have a lettuce,' he
said. It was important to get the goat to
calm down.

Paul looped the rope over one arm
and fed the lettuce to the goat, one leaf
at a time. He was squatting by the main
road doing this when a large yellow
Rolls Royce drew up just beside him. It
was driven by a chauffeur, and in the
back was Marigold Melrose in a big
white hat.

Magically the car window slid down,
and she leaned towards Paul. 'You must

be one of the children in the Fancy
Dress Parade.'

'Yes,' said Paul, 'but they had to
start. They've gone with the
procession.'

She didn't look the same as on the
telly. She looked just as beautiful but
nicer and more worried. 'I'm terribly
late,' she said. 'Where ought I to go?'

'Here,' said Paul. 'I'll show you.'

She stepped down out of the Rolls,
which glided away.

'It's all right,' said Paul. 'They'll come back round. You'll still see them. This is where you're meant to stand to make your speech and start the Fair,' and he showed her the platform in front of the Guide Tent. The goat followed, quiet now.

'That's terrifically helpful of you,' she said, 'and I do like the way you handle that goat. Are you at Fletchley Primary School?'

Paul nodded. She gave him a wonderful smile. 'It must be a good school,' she said.

'Oh, it *is*,' said Paul, and he told her all about the writing display and Mr Wilson being worried about everyone leaving to go to other schools. 'And if there aren't enough children it might be closed down,' he finished.

Too late he remembered that Amanda

was leaving to go to boarding school,
but Marigold Melrose didn't seem put
out. 'That would be a great shame,' she
said.

She looked him up and down
carefully. 'Now, don't tell me, let me
guess . . . you're . . . um . . .' She
looked at the goat. 'I know! Great Big
Billy Goat Gruff and the Troll!' She
dropped her voice to a growl. 'I am a
troll and I live in a hole!'

Paul laughed. She had put on a troll
face. He kept quiet about the elf, he

much preferred the idea of a troll. But he had to be honest about the goat. 'Actually, it's not a billy goat. It's Heidi's goat. I mean Amanda's. She says she's going to win.'

'Oh?' said Marigold, suddenly riveted. 'What makes her think that?'

'We-ell,' said Paul, 'aren't you her aunt?'

'Yes, indeed I am. But did she really say that, horrid little beast? I've always thought my brother spoilt her rotten. We'll see about that.'

There was a shout from over by the Cross Keys, and two photographers came running towards them. People turned to look, and then came hurrying across the green.

'Here we go,' said Marigold to Paul. 'Don't run away, I'd like to take a look at your writing when this is over.'

Paul's heart sank, but he had no time to worry. At the first flash of a press camera the goat lifted its head and flared its nostrils. Paul held on tight. Another, and the goat backed off the platform, Paul after it. The television crew were laying cables from their van, and the goat danced sideways over them.

Paul looked round desperately for help, but by now only Marigold's hat was visible in a sea of people jostling round her. Paul yanked the goat over to the Guide Tent, pushed it through the entrance and zipped up the flap as fast as he could.

The procession with all the floats came rolling slowly towards them, and every camera was trained on Marigold. When the clapping had died down and there was a hush, Marigold began to speak.

'I want first to thank this young man, who has made me so welcome to your village,' and she held out a hand towards Paul. Speechless, Paul felt himself propelled forward onto the platform with her. She went on to say how pleased she was to be in Fletchley, and what an excellent school Fletchley Primary must be to produce boys as helpful and friendly as Paul.

There was a look of stunned surprise on Miss Hornbeam's face, and Mr

Wilson had his mouth open, but Paul did not see them. His head was spinning and he was dazzled by the television lights. He heard Marigold say that he had a great future working with animals, and that there was nothing like a good local school, she had been to one herself.

At this there was a storm of clapping, and then a pause as everyone shuffled back to let her see all the children in their costumes. There was absolute hush while she looked at each one. The only sound was the clicking of cameras.

And then it happened. From behind him in the Guide Tent, Paul heard a faint tearing sound, and a steady chomping. Beside him Marigold was awarding the first prize to the Dalek, and Paul did not dare move.

He stood in agony through more

clapping, and Mr Wilson's thank you speech. Then everyone surged forward, and Paul heard Marigold say to a scowling Amanda, 'Hallo, I've a little bone to pick with you –' but he did not wait to hear more. He darted to the Guide Tent and unzipped the flap.

There was the goat, standing on its hind legs, front feet splayed against the screen, ripping off the pages of writing. Of Paul's work there was nothing to be seen.

That evening, on the six o'clock television round-up there were not only pictures of Marigold Melrose, there were pictures of Paul with her, at first holding onto the goat and then, later, on his own. The local paper rang to ask him about pet care for a piece on the children's page. Next day Marigold's speech was reported in all the papers, and soon Fletchley Primary became the most sought after school in the county.

As for Paul, his Mum couldn't get over the fact that he'd been on television. She said that as he was so good with goats he could surely have a rabbit all his own, and as soon as Tom Drew's rabbits were big enough Paul went round to get one.

'Oh *Paul!*' said his Dad. 'It's a beauty. What are you going to call it?'

'Marigold,' said Paul.